Big Book of Fairy Tales

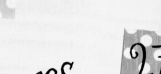

Miles
Kelly

First published in 2014 by Miles Kelly Publishing Ltd
Harding's Barn, Bardfield End Green, Thaxted, Essex, CM6 3PX, UK

2 4 6 8 10 9 7 5 3 1

Publishing Director Belinda Gallagher
Creative Director Jo Cowan
Editorial Director Rosie Neave
Designer Joe Jones
Production Manager Elizabeth Collins
Reprographics Stephan Davis, Jennifer Cozens, Thom Allaway

ISBN 978-1-78209-659-7

Printed in China

British Library Cataloguing-in-Publication Data
A catalogue record for this book is available from the British Library

ACKNOWLEDGEMENTS
The publishers would like to thank the following artists who have contributed to this book:
Francesca Assirelli, Monika Filipina, Sharon Harmer and Kay Widdowson

Made with paper from a sustainable forest

www.mileskelly.net
info@mileskelly.net

Puss in Boots

There was once a miller who had three sons. When he died, he left the mill to his eldest son and a donkey to his middle son.

The youngest son was given the miller's cat. "What am I to do with a cat?" he said. Imagine his surprise when Puss replied, "Give me some boots and a bag and you shall see!"

5

So the youngest son gave Puss some boots and
a bag. Puss went to a field and put carrots in the
bag, then he hid in the grass. Before long, a rabbit
hopped into the bag, tempted by the carrots.

6

Off Puss ran to the palace, where he offered the rabbit to the king as a gift from the Marquis of Carabas. The king was delighted.

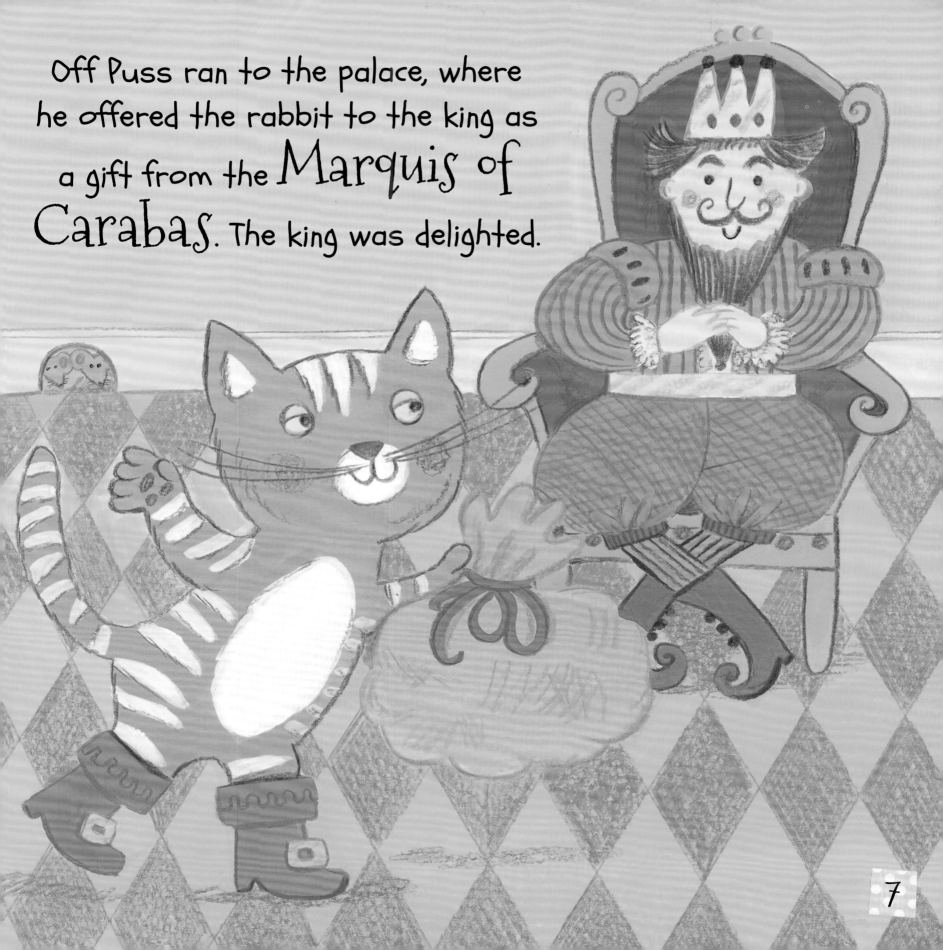

7

The next day, Puss said to the miller's son, "Come to the river and help me fish." Puss knew the king would be driving by in his carriage.

Help!

8

"Quick, get into the water!" said Puss. The miller's son did, just as the carriage passed by. Then Puss hid his master's clothes.

9

"STOP!" cried Puss, and he ran in front of the carriage. "My master, the Marquis of Carabas, has been robbed! Thieves stole his clothes as he swam in the river!"

The king ordered fine clothes to be brought for the miller's son. Then he was invited to ride in the carriage with the king and the princess.

In the meantime, Puss ran ahead of the carriage. He met some workers gathering hay in the fields.

"When the king's carriage drives by, the king will ask who owns this land," said Puss. "Say it belongs to the Marquis of Carabas." Sure enough, this is what happened. The king was impressed.

Bang Bang!

Once again, Puss ran ahead. He came to a big castle where he knew an ogre lived. Puss knocked loudly at the gate and a servant let him in.

14

Puss was taken to
meet the ogre, and
he bowed down low.
"What do you want?"
the ogre growled.

GRRR!

15

Puss was scared, but he said, "I've heard you can do amazing magic Mr Ogre, and turn yourself into any animal. But can you turn into a lion?" The ogre immediately became a roaring lion.

ROAARR!

16

17

18

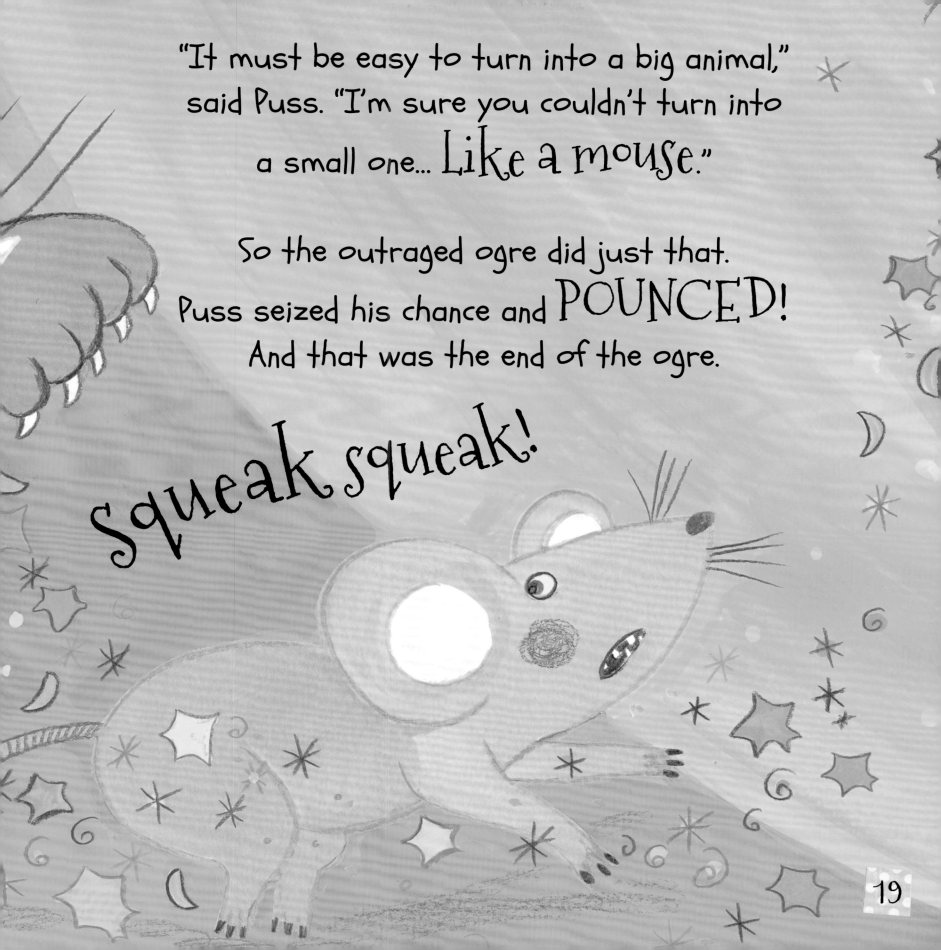

"It must be easy to turn into a big animal," said Puss. "I'm sure you couldn't turn into a small one... Like a mouse."

So the outraged ogre did just that. Puss seized his chance and POUNCED! And that was the end of the ogre.

Squeak squeak!

The servants in the castle were very happy. They had been under the ogre's spell. Pleased to be free, they agreed to become servants of the

Marquis of Carabas.

Suddenly, Puss heard the King's carriage approach.

"Prepare a feast for the king and the Marquis of Carabas!" he said.

21

Welcome!

The carriage stopped and the king stepped out, amazed. "Welcome to the castle of the Marquis of Carabas!" said Puss, bowing low.

22

They all sat down to a huge feast. The miller's son and the princess had fallen in love. The king offered the Marquis of Carabas his daughter's hand in marriage.

The next day the princess and the miller's son were married. Puss was very pleased at the way his plan had worked out.

Congratulations!

25

Puss spent the rest of his days living in luxury – and the only time he ever chased mice was for his own amusement.

Eeek!

Goldilocks
and the
Three Bears

Once upon a time, there were **three bears** who lived in a house on the edge of a wood.

28

There was Father Bear,
Mother Bear and
little Baby Bear.

Every day, the bears had porridge for breakfast. But one morning they found it was far too hot to eat.

"Let's go for a walk in the wood while
the porridge cools down," said Father Bear.

A little girl called Goldilocks was also walking in the wood that day. She had wandered too far from home while playing.

At last Goldilocks came across the bears' house. The door was open, so she went in to have a look around.

Goldilocks saw the three bowls. She tried porridge in the biggest bowl, but it was too lumpy. The medium-sized bowl was too sweet. But the porridge in the smallest bowl was just right.

Too sweet!

Too lumpy!

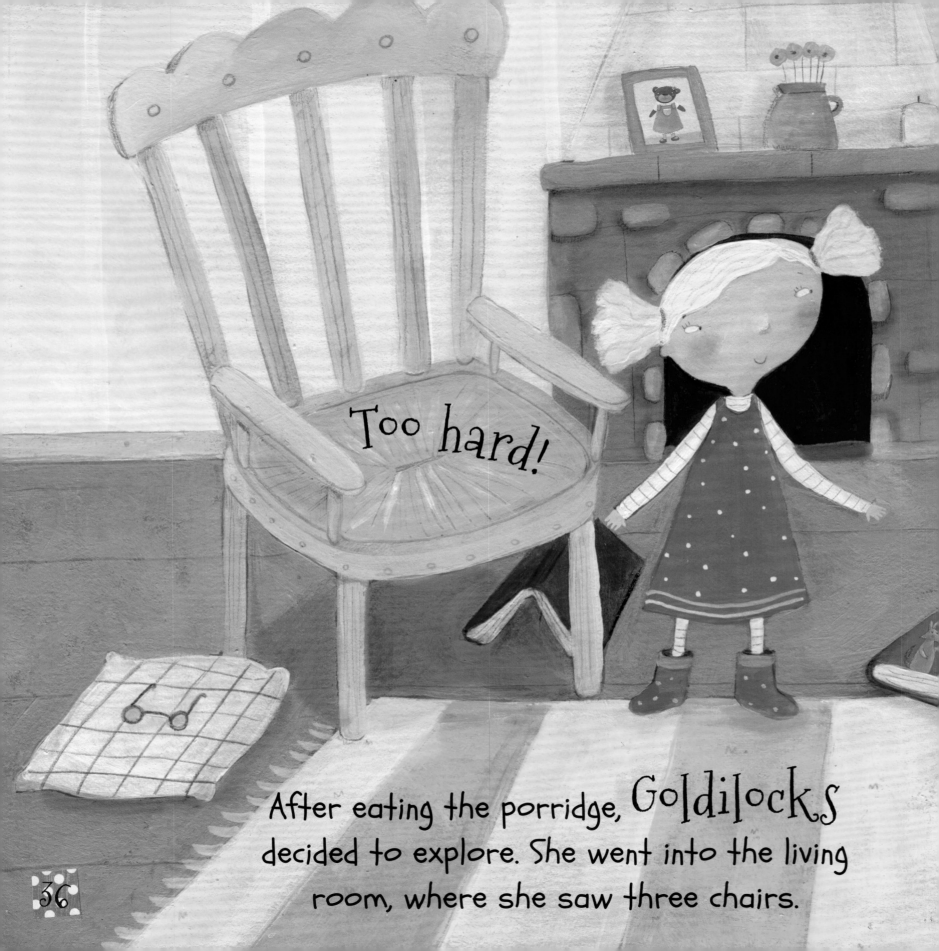

Too hard!

After eating the porridge, Goldilocks decided to explore. She went into the living room, where she saw three chairs.

She sat in the **biggest** chair, but it was too hard. The **medium-sized** chair was too soft. So Goldilocks tried the **smallest** chair.

Too soft!

37

Whoops!

The smallest chair was just right. But all of a sudden... CRASH! it broke into pieces.

All of a sudden Goldilocks felt **very tired.** She went upstairs to find somewhere to sleep.

There were three beds in a big bedroom.
Goldilocks tried each of them, and found
that the smallest bed was just right.

She fell
fast asleep.

41

"I'm starving!"

When the three bears arrived home they were very hungry. But something wasn't right. "Someone's been eating my porridge," growled Father Bear.

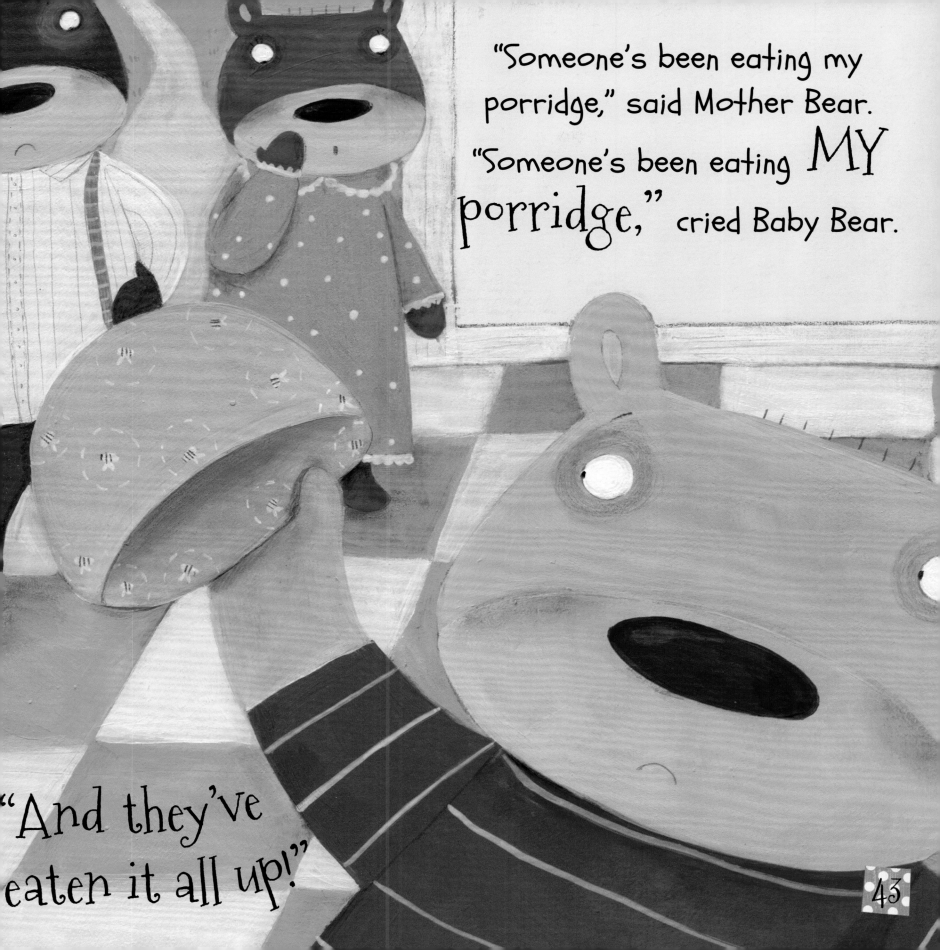

"Someone's been eating my porridge," said Mother Bear.

"Someone's been eating MY porridge," cried Baby Bear.

"And they've eaten it all up!"

43

The bears went into the living room. "Someone's been sitting in my chair," growled Father Bear. "Someone's been sitting in my chair," said Mother Bear.

"Someone's been sitting in MY chair," wailed Baby Bear.

"And they've broken it!"

44

Stomp stomp stomp!

Together, the **three bears** marched upstairs to investigate.

"Someone's been sleeping in my bed!" roared Father Bear.
"And in my bed, too!" cried Mother Bear.

"Someone's been sleeping in my bed," squealed Baby Bear. "And she's still there!" Goldilocks awoke to see the three bears.

48

She let out a loud scream!

AAARGH!

49

Goldilocks leapt out of bed and ran down the stairs. She ran all the way home. And what did the bears do? They made some **more porridge!**

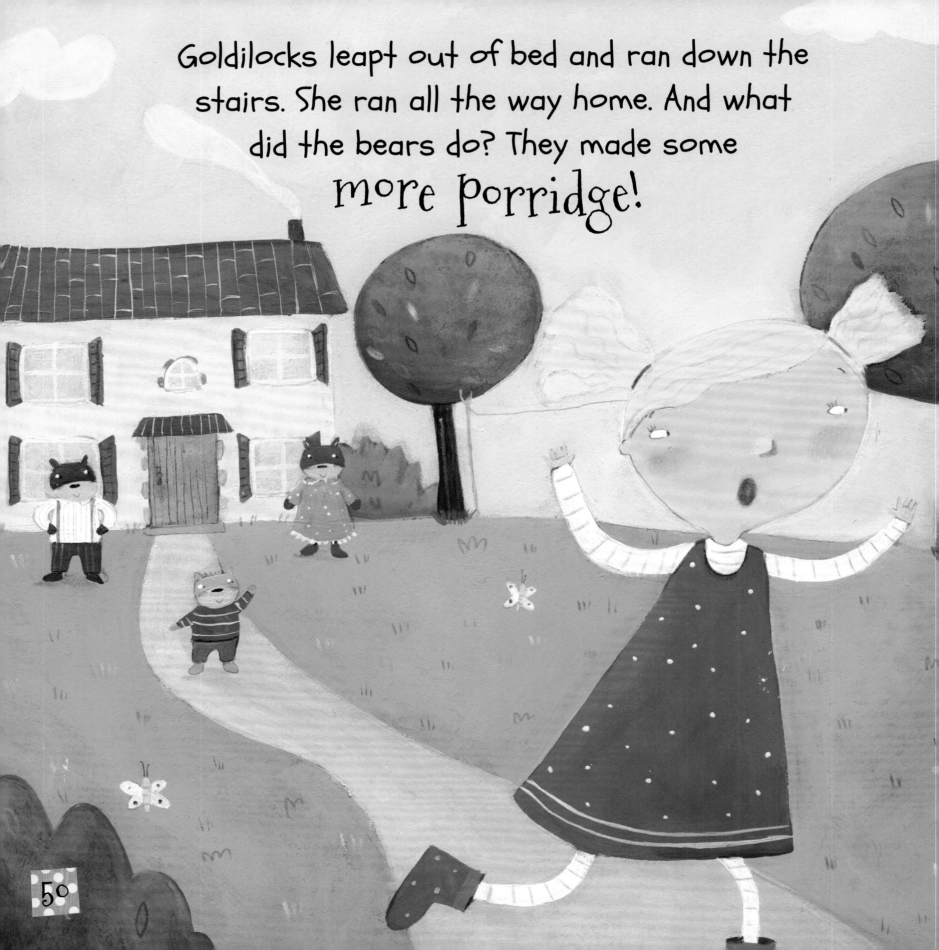

50

The Three Little Pigs

Once there were **three little pigs**. They lived happily with their mother until the day came for them to make their own way in the world.

"Good-bye!"

"Bye Mum!"

"Goodbye Mum!" said the three little pigs.
"We'll call you as soon as we can."

53

They hadn't gone far when the three little pigs
decided to stop for a picnic. "Where are we going
to live?" the little girl pig asked her brothers.

Then one of the little boy pigs saw a farmer with a cartload of straw. "Perfect house-building material," said the little pig, and he bought the whole load.

The little pig soon built his straw house. Suddenly he heard a voice outside say, "Let me in little pig!" It was a hungry wolf.

"Not by the hair on my chinny chin chin!" replied the little pig.

"Then I'll huff and I'll puff and I'll BLOW your house down!"

The wolf blew down the house of STRAW, but the little pig managed to escape.

The two other little pigs carried on their way, until they met a woman with a huge load of sticks. The second little boy pig bought the sticks and built a house.

58

Then along came the big bad wolf. He knocked on the door of the stick house.

"Let me in little pig, let me in!"

But the second little pig said, "Not by the hair on my chinny chin chin!"

"Then I'll huff and I'll puff and I'll BLOW your house down!"

As the house of sticks was blown down, sticks flew everywhere, hitting the wolf on the head.

60

The second little pig made his getaway. He ran off as fast he could to find his brother and sister.

61

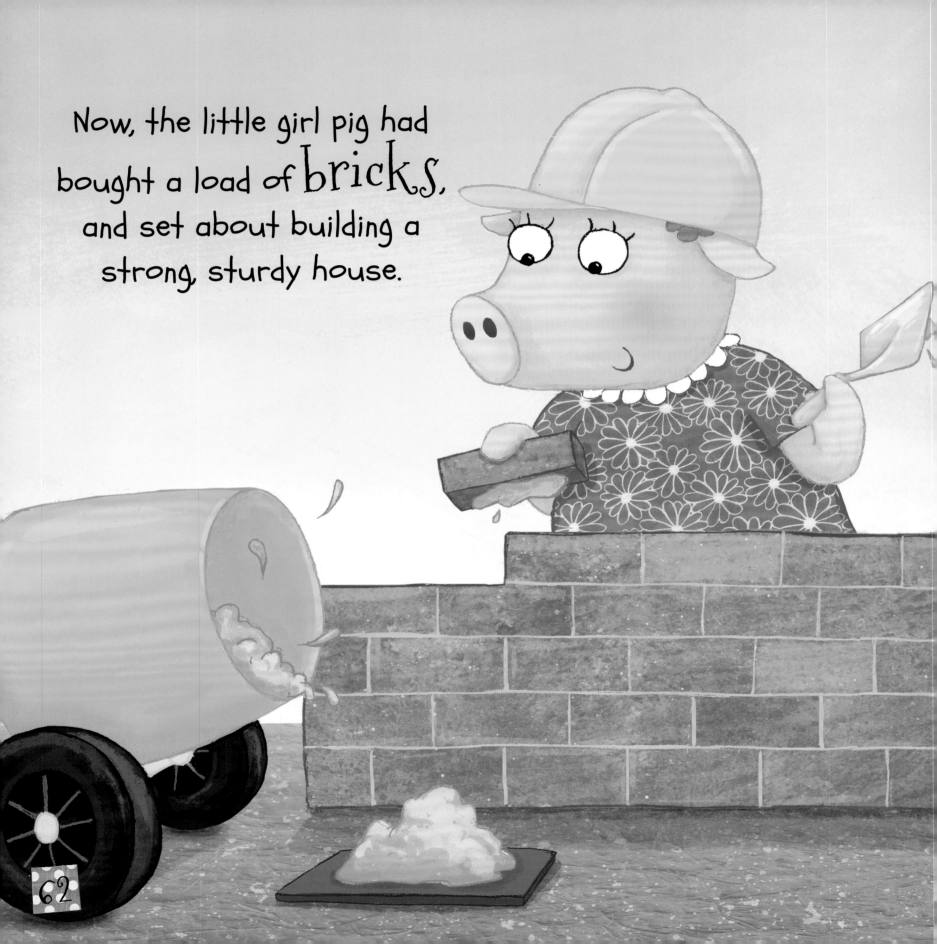

Now, the little girl pig had bought a load of *bricks*, and set about building a strong, sturdy house.

62

Home sweet home!

She worked very hard, and soon the house was ready. The little pig was very pleased with herself.

63

The third little pig settled into her new home. But soon there was a knock at the door. It was her brothers!

Bang bang!

The boy pigs told their sister about the big bad wolf. Together they came up with a plan.

65

Soon there was another knock at the door. The third little pig peeked out of the window. It was the

big bad wolf.

And the wolf huffed and puffed, and puffed and huffed. But the brick house was very strong. Inside, the little pigs put a big pot of water on the fire to boil.

69

"You won't escape!" called the wolf, and he clambered onto the roof and began to climb down the chimney.

"Hee hee!"

70

But the little pigs were ready for him. The huge pot of water in the fireplace was bubbling away.

Suddenly there was a huge
SPLASH as the wolf fell
into the pot of bubbling water.

Splish!

Splash!

Splosh!

72

"Hurrah!" the three little pigs cheered.

"The big bad wolf is dead!"

And the three little pigs lived happily ever after in the house of bricks.

74

Little Red Riding Hood

Little Red Riding Hood lived in a cottage by a wood. One day her mother said, "Your Grandma is ill. Please take this basket of cakes and fruit to her."

76

So Little Red Riding Hood set off with the basket, wearing her red cape. "Don't talk to strangers, especially not to WOLVES!" her mother called.

"Bye Mum!"

Little Red Riding Hood walked through the wood. The trees were tall and made scary shadows. Suddenly, a wolf jumped out.

78

"Hello," growled the wolf. "Where are you going?" "I'm taking some cakes and fruit to my Grandma," said Little Red Riding Hood.

79

"What a sweet child you are," said the wolf.
"Why not pick your Grandma some flowers too?"
With that the big bad wolf ran off, leaving Little
Red Riding Hood happily picking flowers.

Little did she know, the wolf had raced ahead to Grandma's house.

When he arrived, the wolf
knocked softly on the door.
"Let me in Grandma," he called.
"I've brought you some cakes and fruit."

"It's me,
Grandma!"

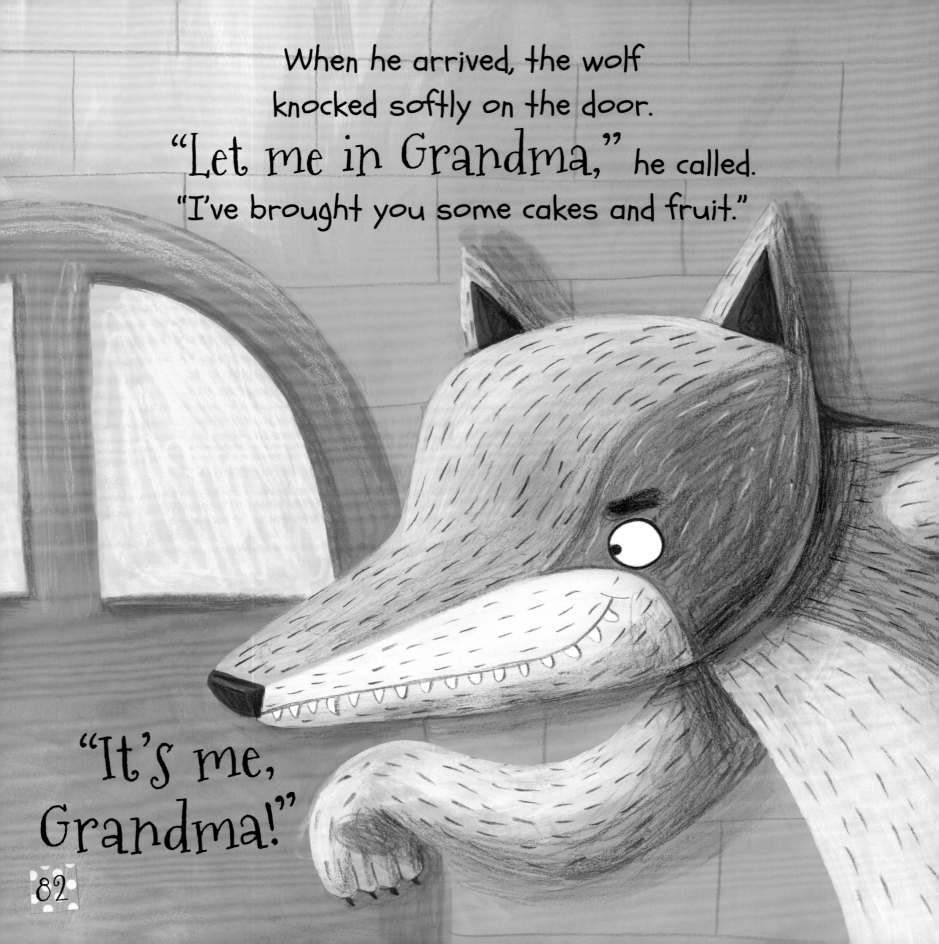

But Grandma wasn't silly. "That's not Little Red Riding Hood's voice," she said. Quickly, she made her bed and hid in the wardrobe.

"Grandma?"

84

The wolf burst into the cottage, but Grandma was nowhere to be seen. So he dressed himself in her nightgown and bedcap and got into bed.

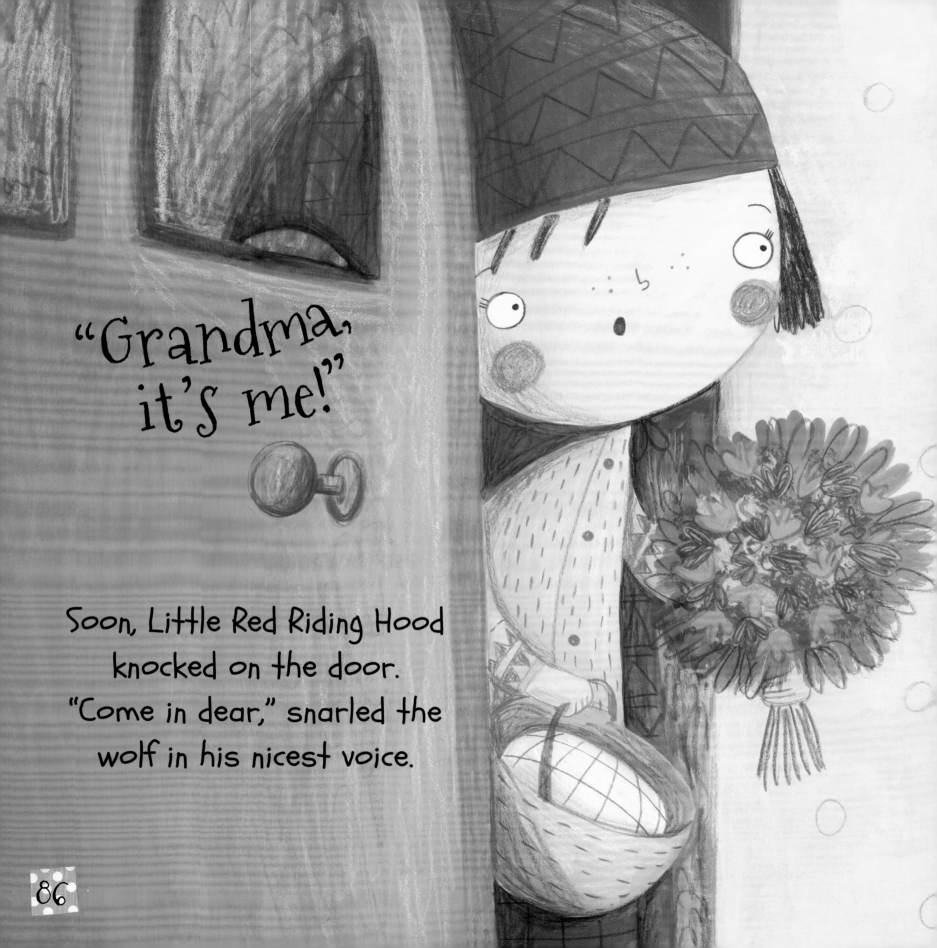

"Grandma, it's me!"

Soon, Little Red Riding Hood knocked on the door. "Come in dear," snarled the wolf in his nicest voice.

86

"Grandma, you look odd!" said Little Red Riding Hood.

"Come and sit beside me dear," growled the wolf.

87

Little Red Riding Hood sat on the bed.

"What big ears you have Grandma," she said.
"All the better to hear you with dear,"
replied the wolf.

"What big eyes you have Grandma."

"All the better to see you with dear."

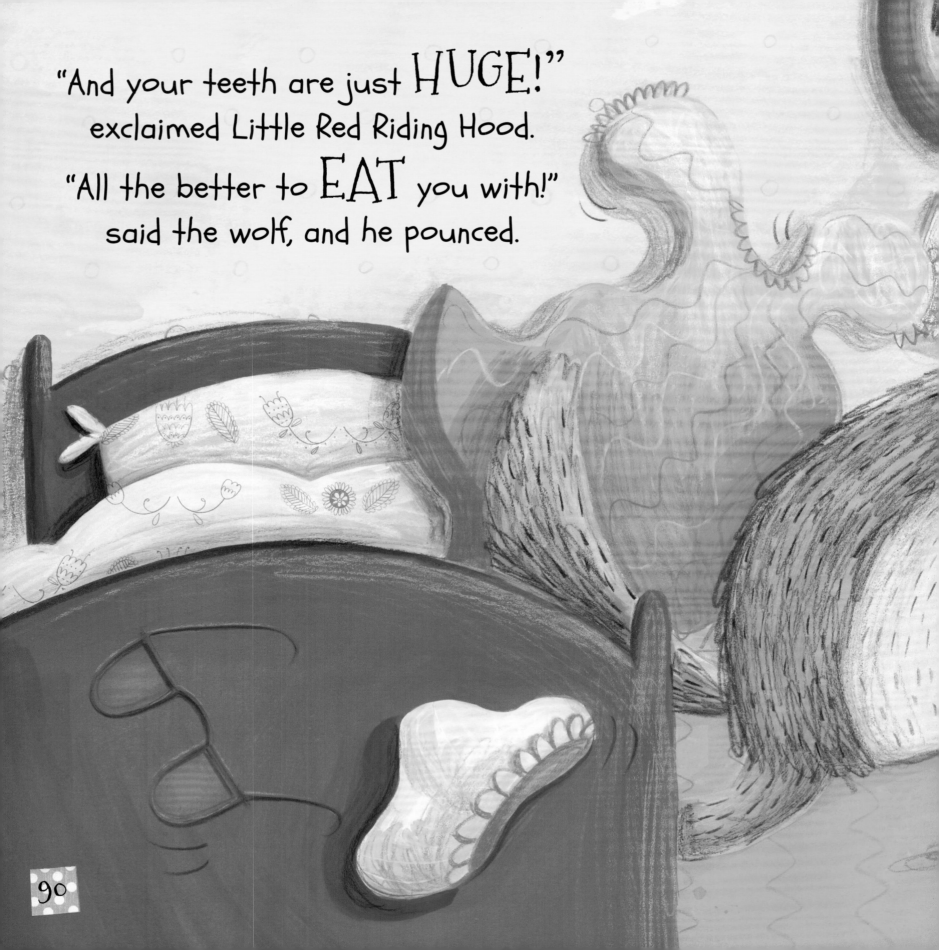

"And your teeth are just HUGE!" exclaimed Little Red Riding Hood.
"All the better to EAT you with!" said the wolf, and he pounced.

90

Bang bang
bang!

Little Red Riding Hood screamed loudly
and ran away. The wolf leapt after her, but
suddenly there was a banging at the door.

Little Red Riding Hood opened the door. There stood a woodcutter who had heard her **screams.**

He raised his axe.

92

With a howl of fear, the big bad wolf dashed past the woodcutter, out of the cottage and away into the forest.

93

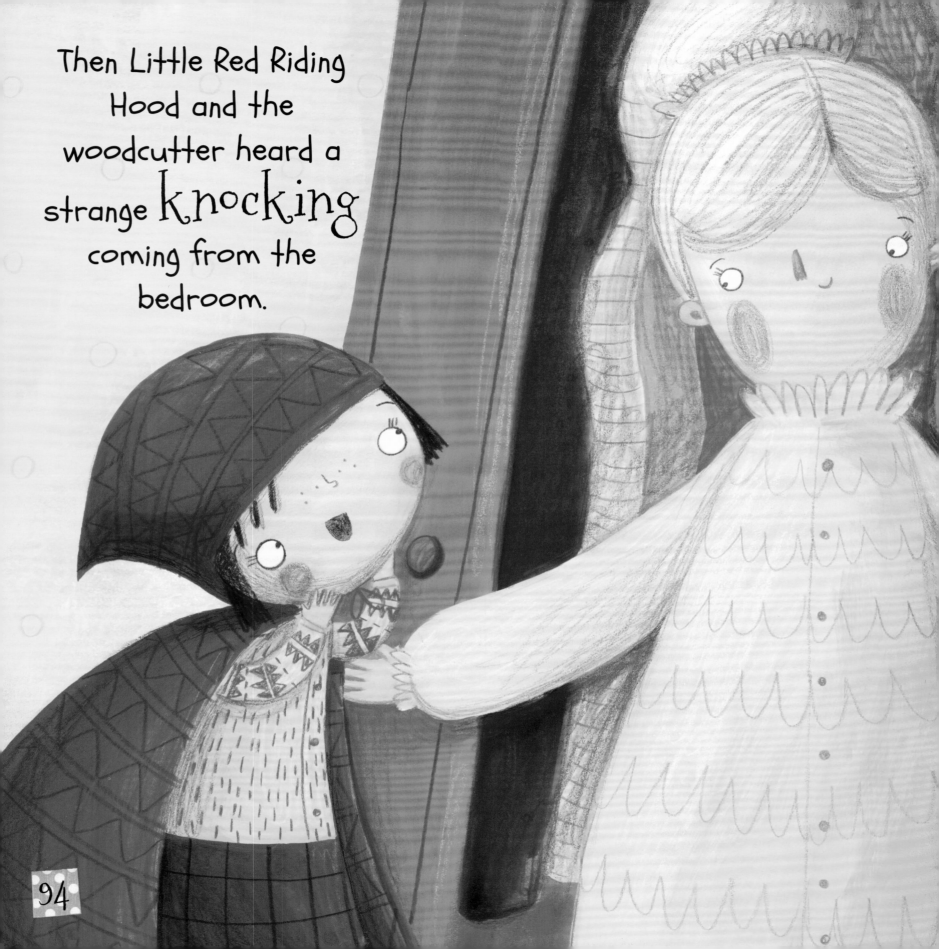

Then Little Red Riding Hood and the woodcutter heard a strange knocking coming from the bedroom.

94

Never again did Little Red Riding Hood talk to strangers. As for the wolf, he kept well away from little girls – especially those wearing red capes!